THE JUDGEMENT
AND
IN THE PENAL COLONY

Franz Kafka

The Judgement
and
In the Penal Colony

TRANSLATED BY MALCOLM PASLEY

PENGUIN BOOKS

PENGUIN BOOKS
Published by the Penguin Group
Penguin Books USA Inc., 375 Hudson Street,
New York, New York 10014, U.S.A.
Penguin Books Ltd, 27 Wrights Lane,
London W8 5TZ, England
Penguin Books Australia Ltd, Ringwood,
Victoria, Australia
Penguin Books Canada Ltd, 10 Alcorn Avenue,
Toronto, Ontario, Canada M4V 3B2
Penguin Books (N.Z.) Ltd, 182–190 Wairau Road,
Auckland 10, New Zealand

Penguin Books Ltd, Registered Offices:
Harmondsworth, Middlesex, England

Published in Penguin Books 1995

Translation copyright © Malcolm Pasley, 1992
All rights reserved

These selections appear in *The Transformation and Other Stories*
by Franz Kafka, translated from the German and edited by
Malcolm Pasley, published by Penguin Books.

ISBN 0 14 60.0178 8

Printed in the United States of America

Except in the United States of America, this book is sold subject
to the condition that it shall not, by way of trade or otherwise, be
lent, re-sold, hired out, or otherwise circulated without the pub-
lisher's prior consent in any form of binding or cover other than
that in which it is published and without a similar condition in-
cluding this condition being imposed on the subsequent pur-
chaser.

Contents

The Judgement
A Story

It was a Sunday morning in the height of spring. Georg Bendemann, a young businessman, was sitting in his own room on the first floor of one of the small, lightly built houses which stretched out in a long row beside the river, hardly distinguishable from one another except in height and colour. He had just finished a letter to an old friend of his who was now living abroad, toyed with it for a while as he slowly sealed it, and then, resting his elbow on his desk, he looked out of the window at the river, the bridge and the rising ground on the far bank with its faint show of green.

He recalled how many years ago this friend of his, dissatisfied with his progress at home, had quite simply decamped to Russia. Now he was carrying on a business in St Petersburg, which after a most encouraging start had apparently been stagnating for some time, as his friend always complained on his increasingly rare visits. So there he was, wearing himself out to no purpose in a strange land; his full, foreign-looking beard only partially obscured that face which Georg had known so well since childhood, with its yellowish skin that seemed to indicate the growth of some disease. By his own account he had no real contact with the colony of his fellow-countrymen out there, and indeed hardly any social intercourse with Russian families, so that he was resigning himself to becoming a permanent bachelor.

What should one write to such a man, who had so obviously taken the wrong turning, whom one could be sorry for but could do nothing to help? Should one perhaps advise him to come home again, to transfer his business here, resume all his old personal connections—for there was nothing to prevent that—and rely for the rest on the support of his friends? But that would amount to telling him in so many words, and the more gently one did it the more offensive it would be, that all his efforts so far had failed, that he should finally abandon them, come back home, and be gaped at on all sides as a prodigal who has returned for good, that only his friends understood things and that he himself was a great baby who must simply do as he was told by these friends of his who had stayed put and been successful. And besides, was it even certain that all the pain that one would have to inflict on him would serve any purpose? Perhaps it wouldn't even be possible to get him back at all—he said himself that he had quite lost touch with affairs at home—and so he would just stay on out there in his remoteness, embittered by the advice offered to him and even further estranged from his friends. But if he really did follow their advice, only to find himself driven under on his return—not as the result of any malice, of course, but through force of circumstance—if he failed to get on either with his friends or without them, felt humiliated, and so became homeless and friendless in all earnest, wouldn't it be far better for him, in that case, to stay abroad as he was? Could one really suppose, in the circumstances, that he would make a success of life back here?

For these reasons it was impossible, assuming one wanted to keep up the correspondence with him at all, to send him any real news such as could be given unhesitatingly to even the most distant acquaintance. It was now more than three years since his friend had last been home, and he attributed this rather lamely to the uncertain political situation in Russia, which apparently was such as to forbid even the briefest absence of a small businessman while it permitted hundreds of thousands of Russians to travel around the world without a qualm. Precisely in the course of these last three years, however, Georg's own life had changed a lot. News of the death of Georg's mother—this had occurred some two years back, since when he and his aged father had kept house together—was something that had still reached his friend, and from the dry wording of his letter of condolence one could only conclude that the grief caused by such an event was impossible to imagine at a distance. Since then, in any case, Georg had applied himself to his business with greater determination, just as to everything else. Perhaps it was that his father, by insisting on running the business in his own way, had prevented him from taking any initiative of his own during his mother's lifetime, perhaps since her death his father, while still active in the business, had kept himself more in the background, perhaps—indeed this was highly probable—a series of fortunate accidents had played a far more important part, at all events the business had developed in a most unexpected way during these two years, the staff had had to be doubled, the turnover had increased fivefold and a further improvement undoubtedly lay ahead.

But Georg's friend had no inkling of this change. Earlier on he had tried—perhaps the last occasion had been in that letter of condolence—to persuade Georg to emigrate to Russia, and had enlarged on the prospects that were open in St Petersburg for precisely Georg's line of trade. The figures were minimal compared with the scale that his business had now assumed. But Georg had felt no inclination to write to his friend of his commercial successes, and if he were to do so now in retrospect it would certainly look peculiar.

As a result Georg merely contented himself with writing to his friend of such unimportant events as collect in one's mind at random when one is idly reflecting on a Sunday. His sole aim was not to disturb the picture of the home town which his friend had presumably built up during the long interval and had come to accept. Thus it happened that three times in three quite widely separated letters Georg had announced the engagement of some indifferent man to some equally indifferent girl, until quite contrary to his intentions his friend began to develop an interest in this notable occurrence.

However, Georg greatly preferred to write to him about things like these than confess that he had himself become engaged, a month ago, to a Fraulein Frieda Brandenfeld, a girl from a well-to-do family. He often talked to his fiancée of this friend of his, and of the special relationship which he had with him owing to their correspondence. 'So he won't be coming to our wedding,' said she, 'and yet I have a right to get to know all your friends.' 'I don't want to disturb him,'

Georg replied, 'don't misunderstand me, he probably would come, at least I think so, but he would feel awkward and at a disadvantage, perhaps even envious of me, at all events he would be dissatisfied, and with no prospect of ever ridding himself of his dissatisfaction he'd have to go back again alone. Alone—do you realize what this means?' 'Yes, but may he not hear about our wedding in some other way?' 'I can't prevent that, certainly, but it's unlikely if you consider his circumstances.' 'If you've got friends like that, Georg, you should never have got engaged.' 'Well, we're both of us to blame there; but I wouldn't have it any other way now.' And when, breathing faster under his kisses, she still objected: 'All the same, it does upset me,' he thought it really couldn't do any harm to tell his friend the whole story. "That's how I'm made and he must just take me as I am,' he said to himself, 'I can't fashion myself into a different kind of person who might perhaps make him a more suitable friend.'

And he did in fact report to his friend as follows, in the long letter which he wrote that Sunday morning, about the engagement that had taken place: 'I have saved up my best news for the end. I have become engaged to a Fraulein Frieda Brandenfeld, a girl from a well-to-do family which only settled here some time after you left, so that you are unlikely to know them. There will be opportunity later of giving you further details about my fiancée, but for today just let me say that I am very happy, and that as far as our mutual relationship is concerned the only difference is that you will find in me, in place of a quite ordinary friend, a happy friend. Furthermore you will acquire in my fiancée, who sends you her warm greetings and will shortly be writing to you personally, a genuine friend of the opposite sex, which is not wholly without its importance for a bachelor. I know there are many considerations which restrain you from paying us a visit, but would not my wedding be precisely the right occasion for flinging all obstacles aside? But however that may be, act just as seems good to you and entirely without regard.'

With this letter in his hand Georg had been sitting for a long time at his desk, his face turned to the window. He had barely acknowledged, with an absent smile, the greeting of a passing acquaintance from the street below.

At last he put his letter in his pocket and went out of his room across a little passage-way into his father's room, which he had not entered for months. There was indeed no call for him to go there in the normal course of events, for he saw his father regularly in the warehouse, they took their midday meal together in a restaurant, and while for the evening meal they made their separate arrangements they usually sat for a while afterwards in their common sitting-room, each with his own newspaper, unless Georg—as usually happened—went out with friends, or more recently went to call on his fiancée. Georg was amazed to find how dark his father's room was even on this sunny morning. What a shadow that high wall cast, rising up on the far side of the narrow courtyard. His father was sitting by the window, in a corner decked out with mementoes of Georg's lamented mother, reading a newspaper which he held up to his eyes at an angle so as to compensate for some weakness of vision.

On the table stood the remains of his breakfast, not much of which appeared to have been consumed.

'Ah, Georg!' said his father, and rose at once to meet him. His heavy dressing-gown swung open as he walked, and the flaps of it fluttered round him. 'What a giant my father still is,' thought Georg.

'It's unbearably dark in here,' he then said.

'Yes, it is dark,' replied his father.

'And you've shut the window as well?'

'I prefer it like that.'

'Well, it's quite warm outside,' said Georg, as a kind of appendix to his previous remark, and sat down. His father cleared away the breakfast things and put them on a cabinet.

'I really just wanted to tell you,' Georg continued, his eyes helplessly following the old man's movements, 'that I've now written off to St Petersburg after all with the news of my engagement.' He drew the letter a little way out of his pocket and let it drop back again.

'To St Petersburg?' asked his father.

'To my friend, you know,' said Georg, seeking his father's eye.—In the warehouse he looks quite different, he thought, how he spreads himself out here in his chair and folds his arms across his chest.

'Indeed. To your friend,' said his father with emphasis.

'Well, you know, father, that I wanted to keep my engagement from him at first. Out of consideration for him, that was the only reason. You know yourself he's a difficult man. I said to myself, he may perhaps hear about my engagement from some other source, even though it's hardly probable in view of the solitary life he leads—I can't prevent that—but at all events he shan't hear about it from me.'

'And now you've had second thoughts?' asked his father, laying his great newspaper on the window-sill, and on top of that his spectacles, which he covered with his hand.

'Yes, now I've had second thoughts. If he's a true friend of mine, I said to myself, then my being happily engaged should make him happy too. And so I hesitated no longer about announcing it to him. But before I posted the letter I wanted to let you know.'

'Georg', said his father, drawing his toothless mouth wide, 'listen to me! You have come to me in this matter to consult me about it. That does you credit, no doubt. But it means nothing, it means worse than nothing, if you don't now tell me the whole truth. I have no wish to stir up matters that don't belong here. Since the death of our dear mother certain rather distasteful things have occurred. Perhaps the time will come to speak of them too, and perhaps it will come sooner than we think. In the business there are a number of things which escape me, perhaps they aren't actually kept from me—I won't assume for the moment that they are kept from me—I'm no longer as strong as I was, my memory's failing, I can't keep track of so many different matters any more. That's the course of nature in the first place, and secondly the death of dear mother was a much greater blow to me than it was to you.— But since we're just on this particular matter, this letter, I beg you Georg, don't lie to me. It's a trivial thing, it's hardly worth mentioning, so don't lie to me. Have you really got this friend in St Petersburg?'

Georg rose to his feet in embarrassment. 'Never mind my friends. A thousand friends can't take the place of my father. Do you know what I think? You're not looking after yourself properly. But age needs to be treated with care. I can't get on in the business without you, you know that perfectly well, but if the business were to endanger your health I'd close it down tomorrow for good. This won't do. We'll have to make a change in your daily routine. A real, thorough change. Here you sit in the dark, and in the sitting-room you'd have plenty of light. You peck at your breakfast instead of taking proper nourishment. You sit with the window shut, and the air would do you so much good. No, father! I'll get the doctor to come and we'll follow his orders. We'll change our rooms round; you shall take the front room and I'll move in here. It won't mean any upset for you, all your belongings can be moved across too. But there's time enough for that, just lie down in your bed for a bit, you really must have some rest. Come, I'll help you off with your things, you'll soon see how well I can manage. Or if you'd rather go straight into the front room you can lie down in my bed for the time being. That would really be the most sensible thing.'

Georg stood close beside his father, who had let his head with its shaggy white hair sink on his chest.

'Georg,' said his father softly, without moving.

Georg knelt down by his father at once, and in his tired face he saw the over-large pupils staring at him fixedly from the corners of his eyes.

'You haven't any friend in St Petersburg. You always were a joker, and you've not even shrunk from playing your jokes on me. How could you have a friend out there of all places! I simply can't believe it.'

'Just cast your mind back, father,' said Georg, lifting his father out of his chair and taking off his dressing-gown as he stood there now quite feebly, 'it must be almost three years ago that this friend of mine was here visiting us. I still remember that you didn't particularly care for him. At least twice when you asked after him I denied his presence, though in fact he was sitting with me in my room all the time. As a matter of fact I could quite understand your dislike of him, my friend does have his peculiarities. But then later on you got on with him pretty well after all. At the time I felt really proud that you were listening to him, nodding to him and asking him questions. If you think back you're sure to remember. He used to tell the most incredible stories of the Russian Revolution. For instance, how he was on a business trip to Kiev, and during a riot he saw a priest on a balcony who cut a broad cross in blood on the palm of his hand, and then raised this hand and called out to the mob. You've even repeated that story once or twice yourself.'

Meanwhile Georg had succeeded in lowering his father into his chair again and carefully removing the knitted drawers he wore over his linen underpants, as well as his socks. The sight of these not particularly clean underclothes made him reproach himself for having neglected his father. It should certainly have been part of his duty to keep an eye on his father's changes of underclothes. Up till now he had not explicitly discussed with his fiancée what arrangements they were to make for his father's future, for they had silently assumed that he would remain on his own in the old flat. But now without more ado he resolved quite firmly to take his father with them into his future establishment. It almost looked, on closer inspection, as if the care he meant to devote to his father there might come too late.

He carried his father in his arms to the bed. During his few steps towards it he noticed with a terrible sensation that his father, as he lay against his breast, was playing with his watch-chain. He could not put him down on the bed straight away, so firmly did he cling to this watch-chain.

But no sooner was he in bed when all seemed well. He covered himself up and then drew the blanket extra high over his shoulders. He looked up at Georg with a not unfriendly eye.

'There you are, you're beginning to remember him now, aren't you?' Georg asked, nodding at him encouragingly.

'Am I well covered up now?' asked his father, as if he couldn't quite see whether his feet were properly tucked in.

'So you're feeling quite snug in bed already,' said Georg, and arranged the bedclothes more firmly round him.

'Am I well covered up?' asked his father once more, and seemed to await the answer with special interest.

'Don't worry, you're well covered up.'

'No!' shouted his father, sending the answer resounding against the question, flung back the blanket with such force that for an instant it unfurled flat in the air, and stood up erect on the bed. He just steadied himself gently with one hand against the ceiling. 'You wanted to cover me up, I know that, my young scoundrel, but I'm not covered up yet. And even if

I'm at the end of my strength, it's enough for you and more than enough. Of course I know your friend. He would have been a son after my own heart. That's why you've been playing him false all these long years. Why else? Do you imagine I haven't wept for him? And that's why you lock yourself up in your office, no one's to disturb you, the master's busy—just so that you can write your deceitful little letters to Russia. But luckily no one has to teach a father to see through his son. And just when you think you've got him under, so firmly under that you can plant your backside on him and he won't move, then my fine son decides to get married!'

Georg gazed up at the nightmare vision of his father. The friend in St Petersburg, whom his father suddenly knew so well, touched his heart as never before. Lost in the vastness of Russia he saw him. At the door of his empty, plundered warehouse he saw him. Among the ruins of his stacks, the shreds of his wares, the falling gas-brackets, he was still just able to stand. Why had he had to go away so far?

'Now attend to me!' cried his father, and Georg, hardly aware of what he was doing, ran towards the bed to take everything in, but then stopped short half-way.

'All because she lifted her skirts,' his father began to flute, 'because she lifted her skirts like so, the repulsive little goose,' and to demonstrate it he hitched up his shirt so far that the scar of his war wound could be seen on his thigh, 'because she lifted her skirts like so and like so and like so, you made your pass at her, and so as to take your pleasure with her undisturbed you have besmirched your mother's memory, betrayed your friend, and stuck your father into bed so that he can't move. But can he move or can't he?' And he stood up quite unsupported, kicking his legs. He was radiant with insight.

Georg stood in a corner, as far away from his father as possible. A long time since he had firmly resolved to observe everything with the utmost attention, so that he should not somehow be surprised, outflanked, taken from the rear or from above. Just now he recalled this long-forgotten resolve, but it slipped from his mind again like a short thread being drawn through the eye of a needle.

'But your friend hasn't been betrayed after all!' cried his father, and his wagging forefinger confirmed it. 'I've been representing him here on the spot.'

'You comedian!' Georg couldn't restrain himself from calling out, then realized at once the harm done, and with starting eyes he bit—too late—on his tongue, so hard that the pain made him cringe.

'Yes, of course I've been playing a comedy! A comedy! Just the word for it! What other comfort was left to your old widowed father? Tell me—and for the space of your answer you shall be still my living son—what else was left to me, in my back room, hounded by disloyal staff, decrepit to the marrow of my bones? And my son went about the world exulting, concluding deals that I had prepared, falling over himself with glee, and stalking away from his father in the stiff mask of an honourable man! Do you suppose that I didn't love you, I from whom you sprang?'

Now he'll lean forward, thought Georg, what if he fell and

smashed himself to pieces! These words went hissing through his brain.

His father leaned forward, but he did not fall. Since Georg failed to approach as he had expected, he straightened up again.

'Stay where you are, I've no need of you! You think you still have the strength to come over here, and that you're just hanging back of your own accord. Don't be too sure! I'm still the stronger by far. Perhaps on my own I might have had to give way, but as it is your mother has passed on her strength to me, I've formed a splendid alliance with your friend, I've got your clients here in my pocket!'

He's even got pockets in his shirt! said Georg to himself, supposing that with this phrase he could make him a laughing-stock in the eyes of the whole world. Only for a moment did he think so, for all the time he kept forgetting everything.

'Just link arms with your bride and try coming my way! I'll soon sweep her away from your side, you wait and see!'

Georg made grimaces as if he didn't believe it. His father merely nodded towards Georg's corner, confirming the truth of his words.

'How you amused me today, coming and asking me if you should tell your friend about your engagement. He knows it all already, you stupid boy, he knows it all! I've been writing to him, you see, because you forgot to take my writing things away from me. That's why he hasn't been here for such years now, he knows everything a hundred times better than you do yourself, he crumples up your letters unread in his left hand while he holds up my own letters to read in his right!'

He waved his arm over his head in his enthusiasm. 'He knows everything a thousand times better!' he cried.

'Ten thousand times!' said Georg, to make fun of his father, but in his very mouth the words turned to deadly earnest.

'For years I've been waiting for you to come out with this question! Do you suppose I concern myself with anything else? Do you suppose I read newspapers? There!' and he threw Georg a sheet of newspaper that had somehow found its way into bed with him. An old newspaper, with a name that was already quite unknown to Georg.

'How long you've delayed before coming to maturity! Your mother had to die, she was unable to witness the happy day, your friend is decaying in that Russia of his, three years ago he was already yellow enough for the scrap-heap, and as for me, you can see what condition I'm in. You've eyes enough for that!'

'So you've been lying in wait for me!' cried Georg.

In a pitying tone his father observed casually: 'I expect you meant to say that earlier. It's not to the point any more.'

And in a louder voice: 'So now you know what else there's been in the world besides you, until now you've known of nothing but yourself. You were an innocent child, it's true, but it's even more true that you've been a devilish human being!—And so hearken to me: I sentence you now to death by drowning!'

Georg felt himself driven from the room, the crash with

which his father collapsed on the bed behind him still sounded in his ears as he ran. On the stairs, down which he sped as if skimming down a slope, he collided with the charwoman who was on her way up to the flat to do the morning cleaning. 'Jesus!' she cried and covered her face with her apron, but already he was gone. Out of the front door he sprang, across the roadway, towards the water he was driven. Already he was grasping at the railings as a starving man grasps at food. He swung himself over, like the outstanding gymnast who had once been his parents' pride. Still holding on, with a weakening grip, he spied through the railings a motor-bus that would easily cover the noise of his fall, called out softly: 'Dear parents, I did always love you,' and let himself drop.

At that moment the traffic was passing over the bridge in a positively unending stream.

In the Penal Colony

'It's a peculiar kind of apparatus,' said the officer to the voyager, and he surveyed the apparatus, which was after all quite familiar to him, with a certain admiration. It seemed to have been no more than politeness that had prompted the voyager to accept the invitation of the commandant, who had suggested that he witness the execution of a soldier who had been condemned for insubordination and insulting a superior officer. Probably there was no great interest in this execution in the penal colony itself. At all events, the only persons present apart from the officer and the voyager, in this deep sandy little valley enclosed by barren slopes all round, were the condemned man, a dull-witted wide-mouthed creature of dishevelled aspect, and a soldier, who held the heavy chain controlling the smaller chains which were fastened to the condemned man's ankles, wrists and neck, chains which were themselves linked together. In fact, the condemned man wore an air of such hangdog subservience that it looked as if he might be allowed to run free on the slopes and would simply have to be whistled for when the execution was due to begin.

The voyager was not much taken with the apparatus, and he walked up and down behind the condemned man with almost visible indifference while the officer made the final preparations, now crawling underneath the apparatus, which was sunk deep in the ground, now climbing a ladder to inspect its upper parts. These were tasks that might really have been left to a mechanic, but the officer performed them with great enthusiasm, whether because he was a particular devotee of this apparatus or because for some other reasons the work could be entrusted to no one else. 'Everything's ready now!' he called out at last and climbed down from the ladder. He was utterly exhausted, breathing with his mouth wide open, and had tucked two delicate ladies' handkerchiefs under the collar of his uniform. 'Surely these uniforms are too heavy for the tropics,' said the voyager, instead of inquiring about the apparatus as the officer had expected. 'Of course,' said the officer, as he washed the oil and grease from his hands in a bucket of water that was standing ready, 'but they mean home to us; we don't want to lose touch with the homeland.—But now just have a look at this apparatus,' he added at once, drying his hands with a towel and indicating the apparatus at the same time. 'Up to this point I've had to do some of the tasks by hand, but from now on the apparatus works entirely by itself.' The voyager nodded and followed the officer. The latter was anxious to cover himself against all eventualities and added: 'Of course faults do sometimes occur; I hope we shall get none today, but one has to allow for the possibility. After all, the apparatus has to operate for twelve hours without a break. But even if faults do occur they are only quite minor ones and can be rectified at once.'

'Won't you take a seat?' he asked finally, pulling out a cane chair from a pile of them and offering it to the voyager; he was unable to refuse. He now found himself sitting at the edge of a pit, into which he cast a fleeting glance. It was not very deep. On one side of the pit the excavated earth had been heaped up to form an embankment; on the other side of it stood the apparatus. 'I don't know,' said the officer, 'whether the commandant has already explained the apparatus to you.' The voyager made a vague sort of gesture; the officer asked for nothing better for now he could explain the apparatus himself. 'This apparatus,' he said, taking hold of a connecting-rod and leaning on it, 'is an invention of our former commandant. I took part myself in the very first experiments and I was also involved in every stage of the work up to its completion. However, the credit for the invention belongs to him alone. Have you ever heard of our former commandant? No? Well, I'm not exaggerating when I say that the organization of the whole penal colony is his work. We, his friends, were already aware when he died that the colony forms such a self-contained whole that his successor, even if his head was bursting with new schemes, would find it impossible to alter any part of the old system, at least for many years to come. And what we foretold has come to pass; the new commandant has had to admit as much. A pity you never knew the former commandant!—But,' the officer interrupted himself, 'I go chattering on, while his apparatus stands here before us. It consists, as you see, of three parts. In the course of time each of these three parts has acquired a sort of popular name. The lower part is called the bed, the upper one is called the designer, and this middle one here, which is suspended between them, is called the harrow.' 'The harrow?' asked the voyager. He had not been listening with much attention; the sun was beating down so fiercely into this shadeless valley; it was hard to collect one's thoughts. All the more did he admire the officer, who in his tight full-dress uniform, weighed down by its epaulettes and hung about with braiding, was expounding his subject with such zeal and for good measure, while still in full flow, giving the odd turn to some screw with his screwdriver. As for the soldier, he seemed to be in much the same state as the voyager. He had wound the condemned man's chain round both his wrists, and with one hand propped on his rifle and his head lolling back was paying no attention to anything. This did not surprise the voyager, for the officer was speaking French, and French was certainly not a language that either the soldier or the condemned man could understand. It was however all the more remarkable that the condemned man was trying his best, despite this, to follow the officer's explanations. With a kind of sleepy persistence he kept directing his gaze wherever the officer pointed, and when the voyager now broke in with his question he imitated the officer by switching his eyes to the voyager.

'Yes, the harrow,' said the officer, 'it's a good name for it. The needles are set in rather like the teeth of a harrow, and the whole thing operates like a harrow, except that it stays in one place and performs with far greater artistry. In any case you'll soon get the hang of it. Here, on the bed, is where the condemned man is laid.—You see, what I want to do is describe the apparatus first, and only then set the actual programme going. Then you'll be able to follow it better.

Besides, one of the cogwheels in the designer is badly worn; it grates horribly when it's turning; then you can hardly hear yourself speak; spare parts are unfortunately hard to come by here.—So here is the bed, as I was saying. It's completely covered with a layer of cotton-wool; the purpose of that will become clear to you later on. On this cotton-wool the condemned man is laid face down, quite naked of course; here are straps for the hands, here for the feet, and here for the neck, to fasten him down. Here at the head of the bed, where as I've said the man lies with his face down to begin with, is this little stub of felt, which can be easily adjusted to push straight into the man's mouth. Its object is to prevent screaming and biting of the tongue. The man is bound to take the felt, of course, since otherwise his neck would be broken by the neck strap.' 'That's cotton-wool?' asked the voyager, leaning forward. 'Yes, indeed,' said the officer with a smile, 'feel for yourself.' He took the voyager's hand and drew it over the surface of the bed. 'It's a specially treated cotton-wool, that's why it looks so unrecognizable; I'll come to its purpose in a moment.' By now the voyager was beginning to feel some stirring of interest in the apparatus; with one hand raised to protect himself against the sun he gazed up at it. It was a large structure. The bed and the designer were of the same size and looked like two dark chests. The designer was mounted some two metres above the bed; both were joined at the corners by four brass rods that almost flashed in the sunlight. Between the two chests, suspended on a steel belt, was the harrow.

The officer had scarcely noticed the voyager's previous indifference, but clearly he now sensed his awakening interest; so he paused in his explanations to give the voyager time to survey undisturbed. The condemned man imitated the voyager; since he was unable to lift a hand to cover his eyes he blinked up unprotected into the glare.

'All right, so there lies our man,' said the voyager, leaning back in his chair and crossing his legs.

'Yes,' said the officer, pushing his cap back a little and passing a hand over his sweltering face, 'now listen! Both the bed and the designer have their own electric battery; the bed needs one for itself and the designer one for the harrow. As soon as the man is strapped down, the bed is set in motion. It quivers, with the smallest and most rapid of vibrations, both from side to side and up and down. You will have seen similar devices in sanatoria; but in the case of our bed all the movements are precisely calculated; the point is that they must correspond with the most painstaking exactness to the movements of the harrow. But it is to the harrow that the actual carrying out of the sentence belongs.'

'And what in fact is the sentence?' asked the voyager. 'You don't even know that?' said the officer in astonishment, biting his lips: 'Forgive me if my explanations may appear disorderly, I do beg your pardon. The truth is that it used to be the commandant himself who gave the explanations, but the new commandant has absolved himself from this duty; all the same, that he should not even have told such an eminent visitor'—the voyager attempted to wave any this honour with both hands but the officer insisted on the expression—'not even have told such an eminent visitor of the form that our sentencing takes, that's yet a further innovation on his part which—,' here he had an oath on his lips, but recovered himself and said merely: 'I was not informed of this; the fault is not mine. In any case I am indeed the one best equipped to explain our kind of sentence, for I have with me here'—he patted his breast pocket—'the relevant drawings in our former commandant's own hand.'

'The commandant's own drawings?' asked the voyager: 'Did he then combine everything in his own person? Was he soldier, judge, engineer, chemist, draughtsman?'

'Yes, indeed,' said the officer, nodding his head with a glassy, meditative look. Then he inspected his hands; they did not seem to him clean enough to touch the drawings; so he went over to the bucket and washed them once again. Then he drew out a small leather folder and said: 'Our sentence does not sound severe. The condemned man has the commandment that he has transgressed inscribed on his body with the harrow. This condemned man, for instance'—the officer indicated the man—'will have inscribed on his body: Honour thy superiors!'

The voyager cast a quick glance at the man; he was standing with bowed head as the officer pointed to him, apparently straining all his powers of hearing to make something out. But the movement of his closed and bulging lips showed clearly that he understood not a word. The voyager had a number of questions in mind, but at the sight of the man he asked only: 'Does he know his sentence?' 'No,' said the officer and was about to continue with his explanations, but the voyager cut him short: 'He doesn't know his own sentence?'

'No,' said the officer again, and he paused for a moment as if expecting the voyager to give some reason for his question, then he said: 'There would be no point in announcing it to him. You see, he gets to know it in the flesh.' The voyager would have said no more, but he became aware of the condemned man's gaze turned upon him; it seemed to be asking if he could approve the procedure described. So having already leant back in his chair the voyager bent forward again and put another question: 'But at least he knows that sentence has been passed on him?' 'Nor that either,' said the officer, smiling at the voyager as if expecting to hear further strange communications from him. 'But surely,' said the voyager, wiping his brow, 'do you mean that the man still doesn't know how his defence was received?' 'He has had no opportunity to defend himself,' said the officer, looking in another direction, as if he were talking to himself and wished to spare the voyager the embarrassment of being told such self-evident things. 'But he must have had the opportunity to defend himself,' said the voyager, and rose from his seat.

The officer perceived that he was in danger of being held up for a long time in his explanation of the apparatus; he therefore went over to the voyager, linked arms with him and pointed to the condemned man, who stood stiffly to attention now that he had so obviously become the centre of interest—the soldier also gave a tug to the chain—and said: 'The situation is as follows. Here in the penal colony I have been appointed as judge. Despite my youth. For I was the former commandant's assistant in all penal matters and I also know the apparatus better than anyone else. The principle on which I base my decisions is this: guilt is always beyond question. Other courts cannot follow this principle since they are composed of more than one member, and furthermore they have higher courts above them. Here that is not the case, or at least it was not so in the time of our former commandant. Admittedly the new one has shown signs of wishing to interfere with my judgements, but hitherto I have succeeded in warding him off and I shall continue to do so.— You wanted to have this particular case explained; it is quite simple, as they all are. A captain reported to me this morning that this man, who is assigned to him as a servant and sleeps outside his door, had been asleep on duty. It is his duty, you see, to get up every time the hour strikes and salute the captain's door. Certainly no onerous duty, and a necessary one, for he must remain alert both to guard and to wait on his master. Last night the captain wished to ascertain whether the servant was performing his duty. On the stroke of two he opened the door and found him curled up asleep. He fetched his horsewhip and struck him across the face. Instead of then getting up and begging for pardon, the man seized his master by the legs, shook him and yelled: "Throw away that whip or I'll gobble you up."—Those are the facts of the case. The captain came to me an hour ago; I wrote down his statement and at once appended the sentence. Then I had the man put in chains. That was all very simple. If I had first summoned the man and interrogated him it would only have led to confusion. He would have lied; if I had succeeded in refuting these lies he would have replaced them with fresh lies, and so forth. But as it is I've got him and I won't let him go.—Is everything now clear? But time's getting on, the execution ought to be starting and I still haven't finished explaining the apparatus.' Pressing the voyager to resume his seat, he went back to the apparatus and began: 'As you can see, the shape of the harrow corresponds to the human form; here is the harrow for the trunk, here are the harrows for the legs. Reserved for the head is just this one small engraver. Is that clear to you now?' He bent forward amiably towards the voyager, willing to provide the most comprehensive explanations.

The voyager studied the harrow with a frown. The information about the judicial process had failed to satisfy him. All the same, he had to remind himself that this was a penal colony, that special measures were necessary here, and that military procedures had to be adhered to throughout. But he also placed some measure of hope in the new commandant, who evidently intended to introduce, however slowly, a new kind of process that went beyond this officer's limited understanding. Pursuing this line of thought the voyager asked: 'Will the commandant attend the execution?' 'It is not certain,' said the officer, put out by the abrupt question, and his friendly expression became contorted: 'That is just why we must lose no time. I shall even have to curtail my explanations, much as I regret it. But of course tomorrow, when the apparatus has been cleaned up—it's only drawback is that it becomes so messy—I could easily add that more detailed points. For the present, then, just the essentials.—When the man is lying on the bed, and this has been set vibrating, the harrow is lowered on to his body. It adjusts itself automatically so that the tips of the needles just touch the body; once the adjustment is completed this steel belt tautens immediately to form a rigid bar. And now the performance begins. The uninitiated onlooker notices no external difference in the punishments. The harrow appears to do its work in a uniform manner. As it quivers, its points pierce the body, which is also quivering from the vibration of the bed. So as to enable anyone to scrutinize the carrying out of the sentence, the harrow is made of glass. Getting the needles mounted in the glass presented certain technical problems, but after numerous experiments we managed it. No effort was spared, you understand. And now anyone can observe through the glass how the inscription on the body takes place. Wouldn't you like to come and take a closer look at the needles?'

The voyager got slowly to his feet, walked across and bent over the harrow. 'You notice,' said the officer, 'two kinds of needles in a variety of patterns. Each long needle has a short one beside it. It is the long one that writes, and the short one squirts out water to wash away the blood and keep the script clear at all times. The mixture of blood and water is then led here into small channels and finally it flows into this main channel which has a drainpipe into the pit.' The officer traced with his finger the exact course that the fluid had to take. When he then, in order to make the picture as vivid as possible, cupped his hands at the mouth of the pipe as if to catch the outflow, the voyager lifted his head, and groping behind him with one hand began to back away towards his chair. He saw then to his horror that the condemned man had also followed the officer's invitation to inspect the harrow at close quarters. He had pulled the sleepy soldier a little way forward on the chain and was bending over the glass too. One could see him searching with a puzzled look for what the two gentlemen had just been examining, and in the absence of any explanation being quite unable to find it. He bent over this way and that. Repeatedly he ran his eyes over the glass. The voyager wanted to drive him away, for what he was doing was probably a punishable offence. But the officer took a firm hold of the voyager with one hand and with the other grabbed a clod of earth from the embankment and threw it at the soldier. The latter looked up with a start, saw what the condemned man had dared to do, dropped his rifle, dug his heels into the ground and tugged his charge backwards so violently that he collapsed; then he stood looking down at him as he writhed about and rattled his chains. 'Stand him up!' shouted the officer, for he realized that the voyager's attention was being seriously distracted by the condemned man. The voyager was even leaning across the harrow without taking any notice of it and was only concerned with seeing what was happening to the man. 'Be careful with him!' shouted the officer again. He ran round the apparatus, grasped the condemned man under the armpits with his own hands, and with the help of the soldier he got him on to his feet after much slipping and sliding.

'Now I know everything about it,' said the voyager when the officer came back to him. 'Except the most important thing,' said he, seizing the voyager's arm and pointing upwards: 'Up there in the designer is the machinery which controls the movements of the harrow, and this machinery is set according to the drawing which represents the sentence passed. I am still using the drawings of the former commandant. Here they are'—he pulled several sheets out of the leather folder—'though I'm afraid I can't let you handle them, they're my most precious possession. Just sit down and I'll show you them from here, then you'll be able to see everything easily.' He held up the first sheet. The voyager would have been happy to say something complimentary, but all he could see was a maze of criss-cross lines which covered the paper so closely that it was difficult to make out the blank spaces between them. 'Read it,' said the officer. 'I can't,' said the voyager. 'But it's quite clear,' said the officer. 'It's very artistic,' said the voyager evasively, 'but I can't decipher it.' 'Yes,' said the officer with a laugh, putting the folder away again, 'it's no copy-book lettering for school children. It needs to be perused for a long time. But I'm sure you'd understand it too in the end. Of course it can't be any simple script; you see, it's not supposed to kill straight away, but only after a period of twelve hours on average; the turning-point is calculated to come at the sixth hour. So the actual lettering has to be surrounded with many, many decorations; the text itself forms only a narrow band running round the body; the rest of the body is set aside for the embellishments. Are you now able to appreciate the work of the harrow and of the whole apparatus?—Well just watch, then!' He bounded up the ladder, set a wheel turning, called down: 'Look out, stand aside!' and everything started up. If it had not been for the grating wheel, it would have been magnificent. As if this offending wheel had come as a surprise to him, the officer threatened it with his fist, then spread his arms in apology towards the voyager and came hurrying down to observe the working of the apparatus from below. There was still something not quite right, something that he alone could detect; he climbed up once more, reached inside the designer with both hands, and then to get down faster, instead of using the ladder, slid down one of the poles and began yelling as loud as he could in the voyager's ear, so as to make himself heard above the din: 'Can you follow the sequence? The harrow begins to write; as soon as it has completed the first draft of the inscription on that man's back, the layer of cotton-wool rolls and turns the body slowly on to its side, to give the harrow a fresh area to work on. Meanwhile the raw parts already inscribed come to rest against the cotton-wool, which being specially prepared immediately staunches the bleeding and makes all ready for a new deepening of the script. Then as the body is turned further round these teeth here at the edge of the harrow tear the cotton-wool away from the wounds, fling it into the pit, and the harrow can set to work again. So it goes on writing, deeper and deeper, for the whole twelve hours. For the first six hours the condemned man survives almost as before, he merely suffers pain. After two hours the felt stub is removed, for the man no longer has the strength to scream. Here in this electrically heated bowl at the head of the bed we put warm rice porridge, of which the man can, if he feels inclined, take as much as his tongue can reach. Not one of them misses the opportunity. I am aware of none, and my experience is considerable. Not until the sixth hour does the man lose his pleasure in eating. At that point I usually kneel down here and observe this phenomenon. The man rarely swallows the last morsel; he simply rolls it round in his mouth and spits it into the pit. I have to duck then, or he would spit it in my face. But how still the man grows at the sixth hour! Enlightenment dawns on the dullest. It begins around the eyes. From there it spreads out. A spectacle that might tempt one to lay oneself down under the harrow beside him. Nothing further happens, the man simply begins to decipher the script, he purses his lips as if he were listening. You've seen that it isn't easy to decipher the script with one's eyes; but our man deciphers it with his wounds. It was a hard task, to be sure; he needs six hours to accomplish it. But then the harrow impales him completely and throws him into the pit, where he splashes down on the watery blood and the cotton-wool. With that the judgement is done, and we, the soldier and I, shovel some earth over him.'

The voyager, inclining an ear to the officer, was watching the machine at work with his hands in his pockets. The condemned man was watching likewise, but uncomprehendingly. He was bending forward a little with his eye on the waving needles when the soldier, at a sign from the officer, slashed through his shirt and trousers from behind with a knife, so that they slipped off him; he tried to catch at them as they fell to cover his nakedness, but the soldier hoisted him in the air and shook the last rags from his body. The officer stopped the machine, and in the silence that followed the condemned man was laid under the harrow. The chains were loosed, and in their place the straps were fastened; in the first moment this seemed almost a relief to the condemned man. And now the harrow lowered itself a little further, for he was a thin man. When the needle-points touched him a shudder ran over his skin; while the soldier was busy with his right hand, he stretched out his left hand in some unknown direction; but it was towards the spot where the voyager was standing. The officer was constantly looking sideways at the voyager, as if trying to read from his face how the execution, which he had by now at least superficially explained, was impressing him.

The strap that was intended for the wrist tore apart; presumably the soldier had pulled it too tight. The officer's help was needed, the soldier showed him the broken piece of strap. So the officer went across to him and said, with his face turned to the voyager: 'The machine is so very complex, something is bound to rip or break here and there; but one mustn't allow that to cloud one's overall judgement. In any case, we can find a replacement for the strap without delay; I shall use a chain; admittedly that's bound to affect the delicacy of the vibrations as far as the right arm is concerned.' And while he was fastening the chain he added: 'The resources for maintaining the machine are now severely limited. Under the former commandant I had free access to a special fund set aside for the purpose. There used to be a store here which kept spare parts of every possible kind. I confess that I was almost extravagant in that respect; in the past I mean, not now, as the new commandant claims, but then everything merely serves him as an excuse to attack the old arrangements. Now he has the machine fund under his personal control, and if I send for a new strap the old broken one is required as evidence, the new one takes ten days to arrive and when it comes it's of inferior quality and hardly fit for anything. But how I'm supposed to operate the machine without a strap in the meantime, that's something nobody cares about.'

The voyager reflected: It's always a serious business to intervene decisively in other people's affairs. He was neither a citizen of the penal colony nor a citizen of the state to which it belonged. If he wished to condemn this execution, or even to prevent it, they could say to him: You are a stranger, hold your peace. To that he could make no answer, but simply add that in this instance he was a mystery to himself, for he was voyaging as an observer only, and by no means with any intention of changing other people's judicial systems. But here the circumstances were indeed extremely tempting. The injustice of the procedure and the inhumanity of the execution were beyond all doubt. No one could presume any kind of self-interest on the voyager's part, for the condemned man was unknown to him, was no fellow countryman, and by no means a person who inspired sympathy. The voyager himself had recommendations from people in high places, had been received here with great courtesy, and the fact that he had been invited to attend this execution even seemed to suggest that his opinion of the judicial system was being sought. And this was all the more likely since the commandant, as he had just heard in the plainest possible terms, was no supporter of this procedure and adopted an almost hostile attitude towards the officer.

At that moment the voyager heard a scream of rage from the officer. He had just succeeded, not without difficulty, in thrusting the felt stub into the condemned man's mouth when the man, in an uncontrollable fit of nausea, closed his eyes and vomited. Hastily the officer pulled him away from the felt and tried to turn his head towards the pit; but it was too late, the filth was already running down the machine. 'It's all the fault of the commandant!' screamed the officer, shaking the nearest brass rods in a blind fury, 'my machine's being befouled like a pigsty.' He showed the voyager what had happened with trembling hands. 'Haven't I spent hours trying to make clear to the commandant that for one whole day before the execution no food must be given. But the new moderate tendency has other ideas. The commandant's ladies stuff the man full of sweetmeats before he's led away. All his life he's lived on stinking fish and now he has to eat sweets! All right, one might let that pass, I wouldn't object, but why don't they get me a new felt stub, which I've been begging for these last three months. How can one not be sickened to take a piece of felt in one's mouth which more than a hundred men have sucked and gnawed at as they died?'

The condemned man had laid his head down and was looking peaceful, the soldier was busy cleaning the machine with the condemned man's shirt. The officer went up to the voyager, who in some vague disquiet took a step backwards, but the officer took him by the hand and drew him aside. 'I should like to have a few words with you in confidence,' he said, 'if you'll allow me.' 'Of course,' said the voyager, and listened with downcast eyes.

'This procedure and this form of execution, which you now have the opportunity of admiring, have at present no open supporters left in our colony. I am their sole defender, and at the same time the sole defender of the legacy of our former commandant. I can no longer contemplate any further development of the system; all my energy is consumed in preserving what we have. When the old commandant was alive, the colony was full of his supporters; the old commandant's strength of conviction I do have in some measure, but I have none of his power; as a result his supporters have melted away, there are still plenty of them about but no one will admit it. If you went into the tea-house today, that's to say on an execution day, and listened to what people were saying you'd probably hear nothing but ambiguous remarks. They'd all of them be supporters, but under the present commandant and given his present beliefs they're completely useless as far as I am concerned. And now I ask you: Is the work of a lifetime'—he indicated the machine—'to be ruined because of this commandant and the women who influence him? Can one allow that to happen? Even if one may only have come to our island for a few days as a stranger? But there's no time to lose, there are plans afoot to contest my jurisdiction; meetings are already taking place in the commandant's headquarters from which I am excluded; even your own visit here today seems to me a sign of the times; they are cowardly and send you, a stranger, out in advance.—How different an execution used to be in the old days! The day before the performance the entire valley was already crammed with people; everyone came along just to watch it; early in the morning the commandant appeared with his ladies; fanfares roused the whole camp; I reported that everything was ready; the important persons—every high official was required to attend—arranged themselves round the machine; this pile of cane chairs is a pathetic survival from those days. The machine was freshly cleaned and glittering, I used to fit new spare parts for almost every execution. Before hundreds of pairs of eyes—all the spectators standing on tiptoe right up to the top of the slopes—the condemned man was laid under the harrow by the commandant himself. The tasks that a common soldier is allowed to do today then fell to me, the presiding judge, and I counted it an honour. And then the execution began! No jarring sound disturbed the working of the machine. Many even ceased to watch and lay with their eyes closed in the sand; all of them knew: Now justice is taking its course. In the silence nothing could be heard but the moaning of the condemned man, half muffled by the felt. Nowadays the machine cannot wring from the man any groans that are too loud for the felt to stifle; but in those days a corrosive fluid that we are no longer permitted to use dripped from the inscribing needles. Yes, and then came the sixth hour! It was impossible to grant every request to watch from close up. The commandant in his wisdom decreed that the children should be given priority; of course I myself, by virtue of my office, could always be close at hand; often I would be squatting there with a small child in either arm. How we all drank in the transfigured look on the tortured face, how we bathed our cheeks in the glow of this justice, finally achieved and soon fading! O comrade, what times those were!' The officer had obviously forgotten who it was he was addressing; he had embraced the voyager and laid his head on his shoulder. The voyager was in great embarrassment, he looked around impatiently over the officer's head. The soldier had by now finished his cleaning up and had just tipped some rice porridge into the bowl from a tin. No sooner had the condemned man noticed this when he began, apparently now fully recovered, to reach out for the porridge with his tongue. The soldier kept pushing him away, since the porridge was no doubt meant for later, but it was certainly just as improper that the soldier should stick his dirty hands into it and devour some of it before the condemned man's ravenous eyes.

The officer quickly pulled himself together. 'I wasn't trying to play on your feelings,' he said, 'I know how impossible it is to make those times comprehensible today. In any case, the machine still operates and it is effective on its own. It is effective even if it stands all alone in this valley. And the corpse still falls at the last with the same unfathomable smoothness into the pit, even if there are not, as there used to be, hundreds gathered like flies around it. In those days we had to install a stout railing around the pit; it has long since been torn down.'

The voyager wanted to avert his face from the officer and looked aimlessly about him. The officer thought he was contemplating the desolate state of the valley; he therefore seized him by the hands, moved round to look him in the eyes and asked: 'Can't you just see the shame of it?'

But the voyager said nothing. The officer left him alone for a little while; with his legs apart, hands on hips, he stood still, looking down at the ground. Then he smiled at the voyager in an encouraging way and said: 'I was quite close to you yesterday when the commandant invited you. I overheard the invitation. I know our commandant. I realized at once what he was aiming at. Although he has power enough to proceed against me he doesn't yet dare, but what he does mean to do is to expose me to your judgement, the judgement of a respected foreigner. He has calculated it all carefully; this is only your second day on the island, you did not know the old commandant and his ideas, you are conditioned by European ways of thought, perhaps you object on principle to capital punishment in general and to this mechanical kind of execution in particular, furthermore you are bound to see that the execution is a sad affair, taking place without public sympathy on a machine that is already worn—all these things considered, might it not well be (so thinks the commandant) that you should disapprove of my methods? And if you do disapprove (I'm still speaking from the commandant's point of view) then you won't conceal the fact, for after all you surely have confidence in your own well-tried convictions. On the other hand, you have seen and learnt to respect many peculiarities of many different peoples, so perhaps you may not speak out with full force against our procedures, as you might do in your own country. But the commandant has no need of that. One passing, one merely unguarded remark will be enough. It doesn't even need to express your true opinion so long as it seems to fit his own purpose. He will question you with the greatest cunning, of that I'm quite sure. And his ladies will sit round in a circle and prick up their ears; you might say, for example: "We have a different kind of judicial process," or "In our country the accused is granted a hearing before he is sentenced," or "With us the condemned man is informed of his sentence," or "We have other sentences besides the death penalty," or "We only used torture in the Middle Ages." All these statements are as true as they seem to you self-evident, innocent remarks that in no way impugn my procedure. But how will the commandant react to them? I can see him, our good commandant, pushing his chair aside and rushing out on to the balcony, I can see his ladies streaming out after him, I can hear his voice—the ladies call it a voice of thunder—and what he now says goes like this: "A famous researcher from the West, given the task of examining the judicial system in all the countries of the world, has just said that our own procedure, based on ancient custom, is inhumane. Given this verdict from such a distinguished person, I naturally cannot tolerate this procedure any longer. With effect from today I therefore ordain—etc." You wish to remonstrate, you never said what he is asserting, you have never called my procedure inhumane, on the contrary you regard it, thanks to your deep insight, as the most humane and the most worthy of humanity, you also admire this machinery—but it is all too late; you never find your way on to the balcony, which is by now filled with ladies; you want to draw attention to yourself; you want to cry out; but a lady's hand covers your mouth—and both I and the work of the old commandant are done for.'

The voyager had to suppress a smile; so easy, then, was the task he had supposed would be so difficult. He said evasively: 'You overestimate my influence; the commandant has read my letters of recommendation, he knows well that I am no expert in legal procedures. If I were to express an opinion it would be the opinion of a private individual, carrying no more weight than that of anyone else and certainly far less than the opinion of the commandant, who has, I think I'm right in saying, very extensive powers in this penal colony. If his opinion of this procedure is as clear-cut as you believe, then I'm afraid the end of the procedure has indeed come, without the need for any modest assistance on my part.'

Had the officer understood by now? No, he had still not understood. He shook his head vigorously, glanced briefly round at the condemned man and the soldier, who both abandoned their porridge with a jerk, came up close to the voyager and said in a lower voice, not looking him in the eye but at somewhere on his coat: 'You don't know the commandant; the position in which you stand towards him and the rest of us is—if you'll forgive the expression—so to speak an innocuous one; your influence, believe me, cannot be rated too highly. I was delighted when I heard that you were to be the only one to attend the execution. This directive of the commandant was aimed at me, but now I shall turn it to my advantage. Without being distracted by any false whisperings and scornful looks—which would have been inevitable given a larger attendance—you have listened to my explanations, have seen the machine, and are now on the point of watching the execution. No doubt your judgment is already firm; should any trifling doubts still remain, the sight of the execution will remove them. And now I appeal to you: give me your help against the commandant!'

The voyager let him go no further. 'But how could I do that,' he cried, 'that's quite impossible. I can no more help you than I can damage your interests.'

'You can,' said the officer. The voyager noticed with some alarm that the officer was clenching his fist. 'You can,' repeated the officer with even greater insistence. 'I have a plan that is bound to succeed. You believe the influence you have is not enough. I know that it is. But even granted you are right, surely it is necessary to try all means, even possibly inadequate ones, in order to preserve the old system? So let me tell you my plan. If it is to succeed, the most important thing is for you to say as little as possible about your verdict on the procedure in the colony today. Unless you are asked directly you should on no account express an opinion; but what you do say must be brief and non-committal; it should appear that you find it hard to discuss the matter, that you feel embittered, that if you were to speak openly you would almost start cursing and swearing. I'm not asking you to tell lies; not at all; you should simply give brief answers, such as: "Yes, I witnessed the execution," or "Yes, I heard all the explanations." Just that, nothing more. Your bitterness, which we want them to recognize, is of course amply justified, but not in the way the commandant imagines. He will naturally misunderstand it completely and interpret it to suit his own book. That's what my plan depends on. Tomorrow there's to be a great meeting of all the high administrative officials at the commandant's headquarters, with the commandant himself presiding. Of course the commandant has succeeded in turning all such meetings into public spectacles. He has had a gallery built that is always packed with spectators. I am forced to take part in the discussions although they make me shudder with disgust. Now at all events you are sure to be invited to this meeting; if you act today according to my plan the invitation will become an urgent request. But if for some mysterious reason you aren't invited, you'll have to ask for an invitation; there'll be no doubt about your getting one then. So there you are tomorrow, sitting in the commandant's box with the ladies. He keeps looking up to make sure you're there. After various unimportant, ridiculous items brought in merely to impress the audience—it's mostly some matter of harbour works, they always keep talking about harbour works!—the question of our judicial procedure comes up for discussion. If it's not brought up by the commandant, or not soon enough, I'll see to it that it happens. I'll stand up and report today's execution. Quite briefly, just the statement that it has taken place. Such a statement is not in fact usual there, but I shall make it all the same. The commandant thanks me, as is his custom, with an amiable smile, and then he can't restrain himself, he seizes his opportunity. "We have just heard," he will say, or words to that effect, "the report of an execution. To that I should merely like to add that this particular execution was witnessed by the famous researcher who, as you all know, has done our colony the exceptional honour of his visit. Our meeting today is also given greater importance by his presence among us. Should we not now ask the famous researcher how he judges our traditional mode of execution and the procedure that leads up to it?" Applause on all sides, of course; general approval, with no one more vociferous than I am. The commandant bows to you and says: "Then in the name of us all I put that question to you." And now you step forward to the parapet. Be sure to place your hands where everyone can see them, or the ladies will take hold of them and play with your fingers.—And now at last you speak out. I don't know how I shall endure the tension of the hours waiting for that moment. In your speech you must set yourself no limits, let the truth ring out, lean out over the parapet and bawl, yes indeed, bawl out your conclusions, your unshakeable conclusions to the commandant. But perhaps you don't wish to do that, it's not in keeping with your character, perhaps in your country people behave differently in such situations, very well then, that too will be quite sufficient, don't even stand up, just say a few words, whisper them just loud enough to reach the ears of the officials below, that will suffice, you don't even need to mention the lack of public interest in the execution, the grating wheel, the broken strap, the revolting felt, all the rest you can leave to me, and believe me, if my speech doesn't drive him out of the hall, it will force him to his knees, so that he has to confess: Old commandant, to your power I bow.— That is my plan; are you willing to help me carry it out? But of course you are willing, more than that, you must.' And the officer seized the voyager by both arms and looked him in the face with heaving breast. He had shouted his closing words so loud that even the soldier and the condemned man had begun to take notice; though they could understand nothing they stopped eating for a moment and looked across, chewing, at the voyager.

The answer that he must give had been clear to the voyager from the very beginning; he had experienced too much in his lifetime for him to falter here; he was fundamentally honourable and without fear. All the same he did now hesitate, at the sight of the soldier and the condemned man, for a fleeting moment. But then he said, as he had to: 'No.' The officer blinked several times but kept his eyes fixed upon him. 'Do you want me to explain?' asked the voyager. The officer nodded silently. 'I am an opponent of this procedure,' the voyager now said, 'even before you took me into your confidence—a confidence that I shall of course in no circumstances abuse—I had already been considering whether I should be justified in taking a stand against this procedure, and whether an intervention on my part would have even the remotest chance of success. It was clear to me who I must turn to in the first place: it was the commandant, of course. You made this even clearer, which is not to say that you helped to strengthen my resolve; on the contrary I can sympathize with your sincere conviction, even though it cannot influence my judgement.'

The officer remained silent, turned towards the machine, grasped one of the brass rods and then, leaning back a little, looked up at the designer as if to check that all was in order. The soldier and the condemned man seemed to have struck up a friendship; the condemned man was making signs to the soldier, difficult though this was because of the tightness of the straps; the soldier was bending down to him; the condemned man whispered something to him and the soldier nodded.

The voyager followed the officer and said: 'You don't yet know what I intend to do. I am certainly going to tell the commandant what I think of the procedure, but I shall do so privately, not at a public meeting; nor shall I be staying here long enough to be called into any meeting; I'm sailing early tomorrow morning or at least going aboard my ship.'

It did not look as if the officer had been listening. 'So the procedure hasn't convinced you?' he murmured, smiling as an old man smiles at the nonsense of a child and pursues his own real thoughts behind that smile.

'Then the time has come,' he said at last, and looked suddenly at the voyager with a light in his eyes that seemed to hold a kind of summons, some call to participate.

'The time for what?' asked the voyager uneasily, but he got no answer.

'You are free,' said the officer to the condemned man in his native tongue. The man did not believe it at first. 'You're free, I tell you,' said the officer. For the first time the face of the condemned man came fully to life. Was it the truth? Was it just a whim of the officer's that might pass? Had the foreign visitor secured his pardon? What could it be? So his face seemed to be asking. But not for long. Whatever it might be, he intended to be really free if he could, and he began to shake himself about as far as the harrow allowed.

'You'll tear my straps,' shouted the officer, 'keep still!

We're going to undo them.' He gave a sign to the soldier and they both set to work. The condemned man chuckled quietly to himself without uttering a word, turning his face now to the officer on his left, now to the soldier on his right, and not forgetting the voyager either.

'Pull him out,' the officer ordered the soldier. A certain amount of care was needed in doing so because of the harrow. The condemned man already had a number of minor lacerations on his back as a result of his impatience.

But from now on the officer hardly paid any further attention to him. He went up to the voyager, took out his little leather folder again, leafed through it and eventually found the sheet he was looking for, which he showed to the voyager. 'Read it,' he said. 'I can't,' said the voyager, 'I've already told you I can't read those scripts.' 'Just look at it carefully,' said the officer, coming to the voyager's side so as to read with him. When that proved of no use either he began tracing in the air with his little finger, which he held well above the paper as if this must on no account be touched, trying in this way to make it easier for the voyager to read. And the voyager did make every effort, for he wanted to please the officer in this respect at least, but he found it impossible. Now the officer began to spell out the writing letter by letter and then he read it out again as a whole. ' "Be just!"—that's what it says,' he declared, 'surely you can read it now.' The voyager bent down so close over the paper that the officer moved it further away for fear of his touching it; the voyager said nothing more, but it was obvious that he had still been unable to read it. ' "Be just!"—that's what it says,' the officer repeated. 'Maybe,' said the voyager, 'I'm prepared to believe you.' 'Very good, then,' said the officer, at least partly satisfied, and climbed up the ladder with the sheet; with great care he inserted the sheet in the designer and then he appeared to be rearranging the entire machinery; it was a most laborious business, evidently involving the very smallest of the wheels, at times the officer's head disappeared completely inside the designer so closely did he have to examine the mechanism.

The voyager kept a constant watch on this operation from down below, his neck grew stiff and his eyes ached from the sunlight that flooded the sky. The soldier and the condemned man were occupied only with each other. The condemned man's shirt and trousers, which were already lying in the pit, were fished out by the soldier on the point of his bayonet. The shirt was indescribably filthy, and the condemned man washed it in the bucket of water. When he then put on his shirt and trousers both the soldier and the condemned man had to burst out laughing, for of course they had been slit up the back. Perhaps the condemned man thought it was his duty to amuse the soldier, he whirled round and round in front of him in his slashed clothes, while the soldier squatted on the ground and slapped his knees with laughter. However, they did still control themselves to some extent in view of the presence of the gentlemen.

When the officer had at last completed his work up above, he once more surveyed the whole thing in all its parts with a smile, this time slamming down the lid of the designer, which had stayed open till now, climbed down, looked into the pit and then at the condemned man, observed with satisfaction that he had extracted his clothes, went over then to the bucket of water to wash his hands, noticed too late the revolting filth, which was sad that he was now quite unable to wash them, plunged them finally—this alternative did not satisfy him, but he had to accept it—into the sand, whereupon he stood up and began to unbutton the coat of his uniform. As he did so, there at once fell into his hands the two ladies' handkerchiefs that he had stuffed under his collar. 'Here you are, your handkerchiefs,' he said, and tossed them over to the condemned man. And to the voyager he said in explanation: 'Presents from the ladies.'

Despite the evident haste with which he took off his uniform coat and then undressed completely, he nevertheless handled each piece of clothing with the greatest care, even running his fingers specially over the silver braid of his tunic and shaking a tassel into place. But all this care was hardly in keeping with the fact that no sooner was he finished with each piece of clothing when he flung it at once, with an indignant jerk, into the pit. The last thing that was left to him was his short sword with its belt. He drew it out of its scabbard, broke it in pieces, then gathered everything together, the bits of sword, the scabbard and the belt, and hurled them all from him so violently that they clanged together in the pit below.

Now he stood there naked. The voyager bit his lips and said nothing. He knew what was going to happen, but he had no right to hinder the officer in any way. If the judicial procedure that was so dear to the officer's heart was really on the point of being abolished—possibly as a result of the voyager's own intervention, to which he felt himself committed—then the officer was now acting perfectly rightly; the voyager would have acted no differently in his place.

The soldier and the condemned man understood nothing at first, to begin with they were not even watching. The condemned man was filled with glee at getting his handkerchiefs back, but he was not allowed to enjoy them for long, for the soldier snatched them away from him with a quick, unforeseeable swoop. Now the condemned man in turn tried to pull the handkerchiefs out from under the soldier's belt where the latter had tucked them away for safety, but the soldier was on his guard. And so they struggled with each other, half in fun. Not until the officer was quite naked did they begin to take notice. The condemned man in particular seemed to have been struck with the sense of some drastic reversal. What had been happening to him was now happening to the officer. Perhaps it would go on like that to the bitter end. Presumably the foreign visitor had given the order. This was vengeance, then. Without himself having suffered to the end, he was going to be revenged to the end. A broad, silent grin appeared on his face now, and there it stayed.

The officer, however, had turned to the machine. It had been clear enough earlier that he understood the machine well, but now it was almost staggering to see how he handled it and how it obeyed him. He only had to stretch out a hand towards the harrow for it to raise and lower itself several times, until it reached the right position to receive him; he merely gripped the edge of the bed and it began at once to vibrate; the felt stub came to meet his mouth, one could see that the officer did not actually want it, but his hesitation lasted only for a moment, he quickly submitted and accepted it. All was now ready, only the straps were still hanging down at the sides, but these were clearly unnecessary, the officer had no need to be fastened down. But then the condemned man noticed the loose straps, in his opinion the execution was not complete unless the straps were fastened, he beckoned vigorously to the soldier and they both ran across to strap the officer down. The latter had already stretched out a foot to kick the crank that would set the designer in motion; then he saw that the two men had arrived; so he withdrew his foot and allowed himself to be strapped down. But now of course the crank was no longer within his reach; neither the soldier nor the condemned man would be able to find it, and the voyager was determined not to lift a finger. It was not necessary; hardly were the straps in place when the machine began to operate; the bed vibrated, the needles danced over the skin, the harrow moved gently up and down. The voyager had been staring at it for some time before it occurred to him that a wheel in the designer should have been grating; and yet all was still, not even the faintest whirring could be heard.

As a result of this silent working the machine positively escaped attention. The voyager looked across to the soldier and the condemned man. The condemned man was the livelier of the two, everything about the machine interested him, now he was bending down, now reaching up, always with his forefinger outstretched to point something out to the soldier.

The voyager found this offensive. He was determined to stay here to the end, but he could not have borne the sight of these two for long. 'Go home,' he said. The soldier might have been prepared to do so, but the condemned man felt the order almost as a punishment. He implored with his hands clasped to be allowed to stay, and when the voyager shook his head and would not relent he even went down on his knees. The voyager saw that giving orders was useless, he was about to go over and chase the pair away. At that moment he heard a noise above him in the designer. He looked up. Was that cogwheel giving trouble after all? But it was something else. Slowly the lid of the designer lifted until it fell open completely. The teeth of a cogwheel came into view and rose up, soon the whole wheel appeared, it was as if some mighty force were compressing the designer so that there was no more room for this wheel, the wheel turned until it reached the edge of the designer, fell to the ground, and then rolled along upright in the sand for a little way before it toppled over. But up aloft a second wheel was already emerging, followed by many others, big ones and little ones and ones that were hard to distinguish, with all of them the same thing happened; one kept thinking, surely at least by now the designer must be empty, but then a new, particularly numerous group appeared, rose up, fell to the ground, rolled along the sand and toppled over. Engrossed in this spectacle, the condemned man quite forgot the voyager's command, the cogwheels completely fascinated him, he kept trying to catch one and urging the soldier to help him as he did so, but each time he drew back his hand in alarm, for another wheel would immediately follow it and give him a fright, at least as it started to roll.

The voyager, on the other hand, was deeply disturbed; the machine was obviously disintegrating; its peaceful action was an illusion; he had the feeling that it was now his duty to protect the officer, since he was no longer able to take care of himself. But while the falling cogwheels had been absorbing his whole attention he had omitted to keep an eye on the rest of the machine; now, however, once the last cogwheel had left the designer and he bent over the harrow he had a new and still more disagreeable surprise. The harrow was not writing, it was just stabbing, and the bed was not rolling the body over but just heaving it up quivering into the needles. The voyager wanted to intervene, if possible to bring the whole thing to a standstill, for this was no torture such as the officer had wished to achieve, this was just plain murder. He stretched out his hands. But at that moment the harrow rose with the body spitted on it and swung to the side, as it otherwise did only when the twelfth hour had come. Blood flowed in a hundred streams, unmixed with water, the water-jets too had failed this time. And now the very last stage failed as well, the body refused to free itself from the long needles, it poured out its blood yet it hung there over the pit without falling. The harrow began to move back to its old position, but as if noticing that it was not yet free of its burden it stayed above the pit where it was. 'Come and help!' yelled the voyager to the soldier and the condemned man, and himself seized the officer's feet. He meant to push against the feet from his end while the two took hold of the officer's head from the other so that he might be slowly detached from the needles. But the other two could not make up their minds to come; the condemned man actually turned away; the voyager had to go over to them and compel them to take up their place at the officer's head. In doing so he caught sight, almost against his will, of the face of the corpse. It was as it had been in life; no sign of the promised deliverance could be detected; what all the others had found in the machine, the officer had not found; his lips were pressed firmly together, his eyes were open and had the expression of life, their look was calm and convinced, through his forehead went the point of the great iron spike.

As the voyager, with the soldier and the condemned man behind him, reached the first houses of the colony the soldier pointed to one of them and said: 'Here is the tea-house.'

On the ground floor of this house was a deep, low, cavernous room, its walls and ceiling blackened with smoke. It was open to the street along the whole of its width. There was little to distinguish the tea-house from the other houses of the colony, which apart from the palatial buildings of the commandant's headquarters were all very dilapidated, and yet the effect it had on the voyager was that of a historical reminder and he felt the power of earlier times. He approached it and made his way, followed by his companions, between the empty tables that stood in front of the tea-house in the street; then he breathed in the cool, musty air that came from the interior. 'The old man is buried here,' said the soldier, 'the priest wouldn't allow him a place in the graveyard. For a time they couldn't decide where to bury him, in the end they buried him here. The officer won't have told you anything about it because of course that was what he was most ashamed of. He even tried a few times at night to dig the old man up, but he was always chased away.' 'Where is the grave?' asked the voyager, who was unable to believe the soldier. At once the two of them, the soldier and the condemned man, ran ahead and pointed with outstretched hand to where the grave was. They led the voyager through to the rear wall, where there were customers sitting at a few of the tables. These were apparently dockers, powerfully built men with short black glittering beards. All were in shirt-sleeves and their shirts were ragged; they were poor, humiliated folk. As the voyager approached a few of them got up, backed against the wall and stared at him. 'It's a stranger,' so the whisper went round, 'he wants to look at the grave.' They pushed one of the tables aside, and under it there really was a gravestone. It was a simple stone, low enough to be hidden beneath a table. It bore an inscription in very small letters, the voyager had to kneel down to read it. It read: 'Here lies the old commandant. His followers, who must now be nameless, have dug him this grave and placed this stone. It is prophesied that after a given number of years the commandant will rise again, and will lead out his followers from this house to reconquer the colony. Have faith and watch!' When the voyager had read this and risen to his feet he saw the men standing round him smiling, as if they had read the inscription with him, and found it laughable, and were inviting him to share their opinion. The voyager pretended not to notice, distributed a few coins among them, waited until the table had been pushed over the grave, left the tea-house and made his way to the harbour.

The soldier and the condemned man had found some acquaintances in the tea-house who detained them. But they must soon have torn themselves away, for the voyager had only got halfway down the long flight of steps that led to the boats when they came running after him. Probably they wanted to force the voyager at the last minute to take them with him. While he was negotiating down below with a ferryman to take him out to the steamer, the pair of them came racing down the steps, in silence, for they did not dare to shout. But by the time they reached the foot of the steps the voyager was already in the boat and the ferryman was just casting off. They could still have managed to leap into the boat, but the voyager picked up a heavy knotted rope from the deck, threatened them with it and so held them at bay.

READ MORE IN PENGUIN

For complete information about books available from Penguin and how to order them, please write to us at the appropriate address below. Please note that for copyright reasons the selection of books varies from country to country.

IN THE UNITED KINGDOM: Please write to *Dept. JC, Penguin Books Ltd, FREEPOST, West Drayton, Middlesex UB7 0BR.*

If you have any difficulty in obtaining a title, please send your order with the correct money, plus ten per cent for postage and packaging, to *PO Box No. 11, West Drayton, Middlesex UB7 0BR.*

IN THE UNITED STATES: Please write to *Consumer Sales, Penguin USA, P.O. Box 999, Dept. 17109, Bergenfield, New Jersey 07621-0120.* VISA and MasterCard holders call 1-800-253-6476 to order all Penguin titles.

IN CANADA: Please write to *Penguin Books Canada Ltd, 10 Alcorn Avenue, Suite 300, Toronto, Ontario M4V 3B2.*

IN AUSTRALIA: Please write to *Penguin Books Australia Ltd, P.O. Box 257, Ringwood, Victoria 3134.*

IN NEW ZEALAND: Please write to *Penguin Books (NZ) Ltd, Private Bag 102902, North Shore Mail Centre, Auckland 10.*

IN INDIA: Please write to *Penguin Books India Pvt Ltd, 706 Eros Apartments, 56 Nehru Place, New Delhi 110 019.*

IN THE NETHERLANDS: Please write to *Penguin Books Netherlands bv, Postbus 3507, NL-1001 AH Amsterdam.*

IN GERMANY: Please write to *Penguin Books Deutschland GmbH, Metzlerstrasse 26, 60594 Frankfurt am Main.*

IN SPAIN: Please write to *Penguin Books S. A., Bravo Murillo 19, 1o B, 28015 Madrid.*

IN ITALY: Please write to *Penguin Italia s.r.l., Via Felice Casati 20, I-20124 Milano.*

IN FRANCE: Please write to *Penguin France S. A., 17 rue Lejeune, F-31000 Toulouse.*

IN JAPAN: Please write to *Penguin Books Japan, Ishikiribashi Building, 2-5-4, Suido, Bunkyo-ku, Tokyo 112.*

IN GREECE: Please write to *Penguin Hellas Ltd, Dimocritou 3, GR-106 71 Athens.*

IN SOUTH AFRICA: Please write to *Longman Penguin Southern Africa (Pty) Ltd, Private Bag X08, Bertsham 2013.*